Story © 1985 by Seishi Horio
Illustrations © 1985 by Tsutomu Murakami

First Printing 1985

Heian International, Inc.
P.O. Box 1013
Union City, CA 94587

Originally published by Froebel-Kan Ltd., Tokyo

Translated by D.T. Ooka

ISBN: 0-89346-246-2

Printed in Japan

The Monkey and the Crab

Saru Kani

retold by Seishi Horio
illustrated by Tsutomu Murakami

Heian

One day, Mr. Monkey and Mrs. Crab went for a walk. Along the way, Mrs. Crab found a rice ball lying on the ground. "Look at what I found!" cried the crab.

The envious monkey looked everywhere to find such a treat, but all he found was a single persimmon seed.

He turned to Mrs. Crab and said, "Mrs. Crab, would you like to trade your rice ball for this persimmon seed?"

"I don't want that useless seed," replied Mrs. Crab.

"But, Mrs. Crab, if you plant this seed, it will grow into a huge tree with lots of sweet, juicy persimmons!" cried Mr. Monkey. "You will get hundreds of persimmons for your one rice ball!"

Mrs. Crab decided that the monkey was right, and she traded her rice ball for the little seed.

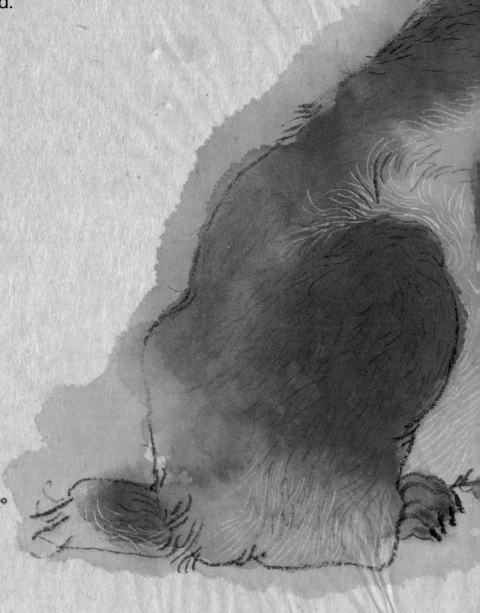

Mrs. Crab took the seed home and planted it. She watered it and fed it every day, singing a song:

"Persimmon, persimmon seed,
hurry and sprout
For if you don't, I'll dig you right out!"

The persimmon seed sprouted very quickly because it didn't want to be dug out of the warm earth.

Then Mrs. Crab sang another song:
 "Persimmon, persimmon
 sprout, small, green,
 and new
 Grow into a tree or I'll
 cut you in two!"
The persimmon sprout grew quickly into a big tree because it didn't want to be cut in half by the crab's claws.

Now as Mrs. Crab watered the tree, she sang this song:

"Persimmon, persimmon tree,
tall, green, and brown
Bear sweet juicy fruit or I'll
soon chop you down!"

In no time at all the tree was covered with ripe, juicy persimmons because it did not want to be chopped down. This made Mrs. Crab very happy and excited.

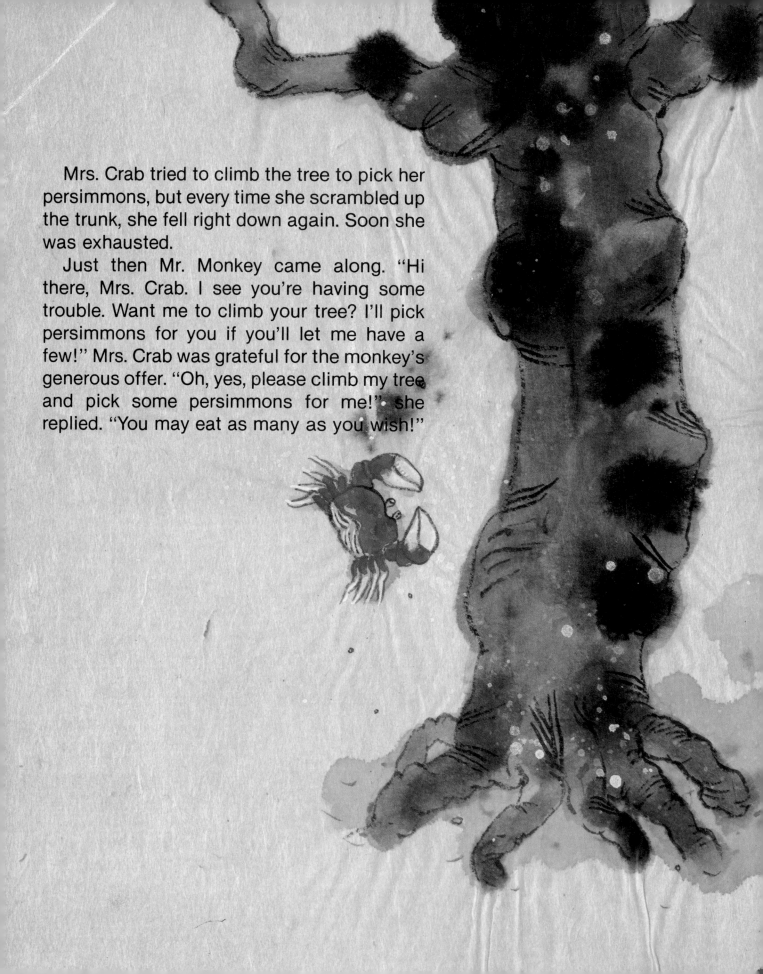

Mrs. Crab tried to climb the tree to pick her persimmons, but every time she scrambled up the trunk, she fell right down again. Soon she was exhausted.

Just then Mr. Monkey came along. "Hi there, Mrs. Crab. I see you're having some trouble. Want me to climb your tree? I'll pick persimmons for you if you'll let me have a few!" Mrs. Crab was grateful for the monkey's generous offer. "Oh, yes, please climb my tree and pick some persimmons for me!" she replied. "You may eat as many as you wish!"

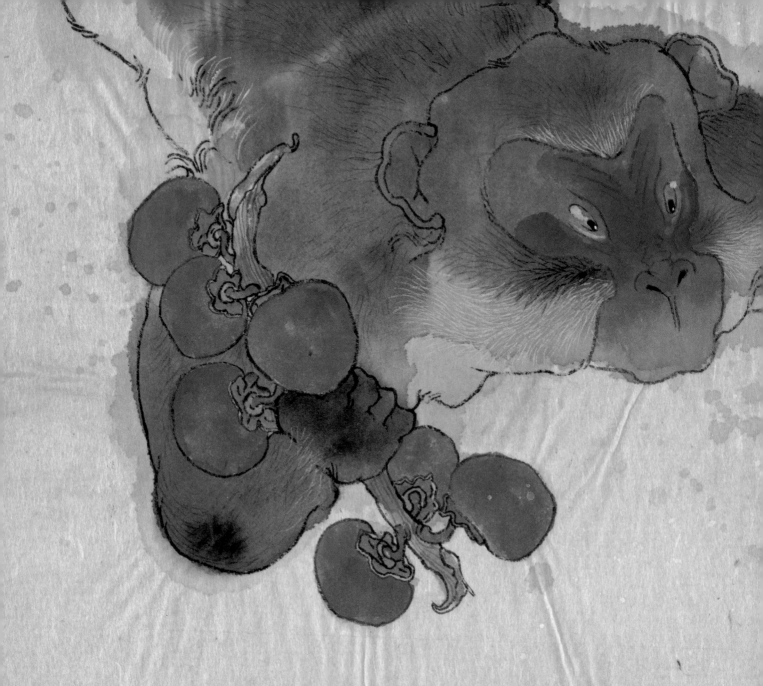

Mr. Monkey climbed the tree and began to eat all the juicy, sweet, red persimmons himself. When Mrs. Crab reminded him to pick some for her, Mr. Monkey shouted down, "These fruits are really mine because they grew from the seed that I found. Why should I give you any of them?"

Then he threw some hard green persimmons down at the waiting crab.

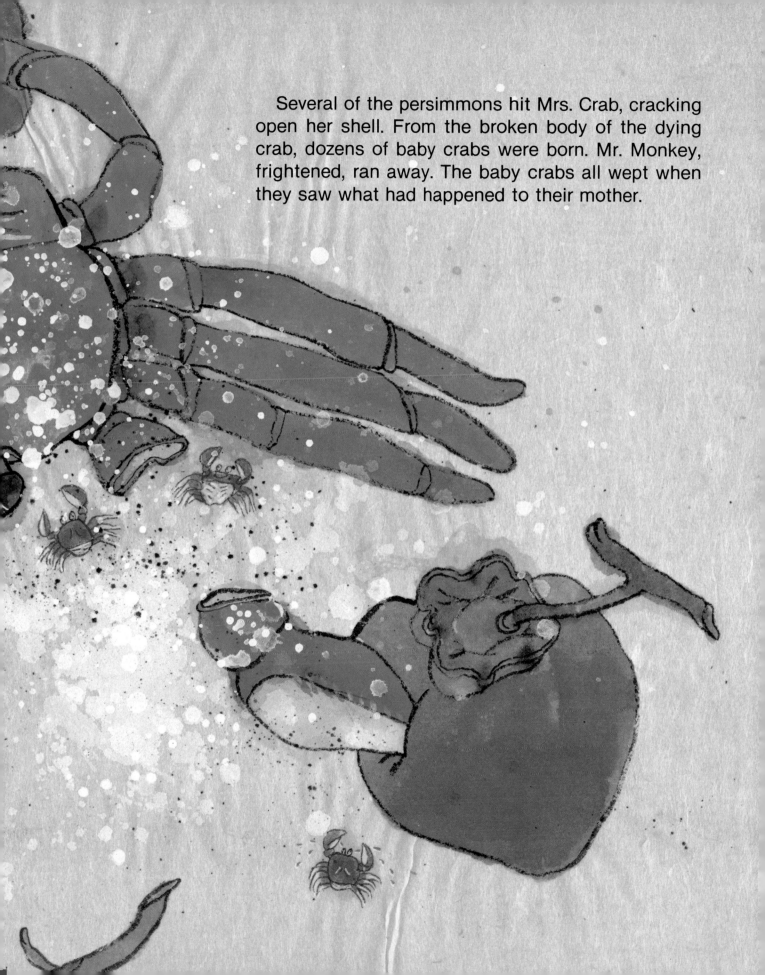

Several of the persimmons hit Mrs. Crab, cracking open her shell. From the broken body of the dying crab, dozens of baby crabs were born. Mr. Monkey, frightened, ran away. The baby crabs all wept when they saw what had happened to their mother.

After a while, Mrs. Crab's children decided to punish Mr. Monkey for killing their mother. As they set out for the monkey's house, they met a chestnut. They told him what had happened to their mother, and Mr. Chestnut became so angry at the monkey that he agreed to help them.

Next, the baby crabs met a wasp. They explained their mission and Mr. Wasp also offered to help them.

Lying in the middle of the road was a cowpat. After the baby crabs told their sad story, Mr. Cowpat also gladly joined their forces.

As they continued on to Mr. Monkey's house, they met a huge mortar. When he learned of Mrs. Crab's cruel death, Mr. Mortar agreed to help them punish the monkey.

And so this strange army marched to Mr. Monkey's house—the scuttling crabs, the rolling chestnut, the buzzing wasp, the sliding cowpat, and the lumbering mortar.

Mr. Monkey was not at home. "Good!" cried the baby crabs. "Let's all hide and surprise him when he returns!" The crabs climbed into the water tub and the chestnut hopped into the fireplace. The wasp hovered quietly just under the eaves. The cowpat sat himself down outside the door while the mortar hid in the rafters.

Soon Mr. Monkey returned home. "Brrr! I'm so cold!" he shivered as he sat down next to the fire, trying to warm himself.

"Boom!" Out of the fire popped the red-hot
Mr. Chestnut, hitting the monkey on the nose.
"Ouch! Ouch! Ouch!" cried Mr. Monkey,
heading for the water tub to cool his burning
face.

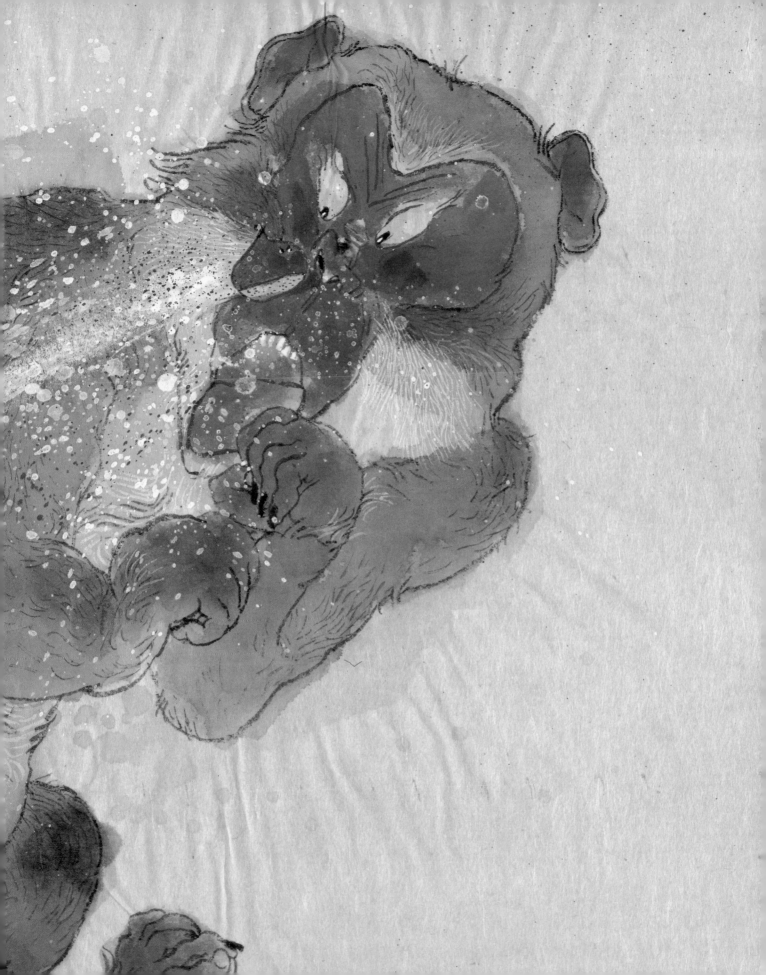

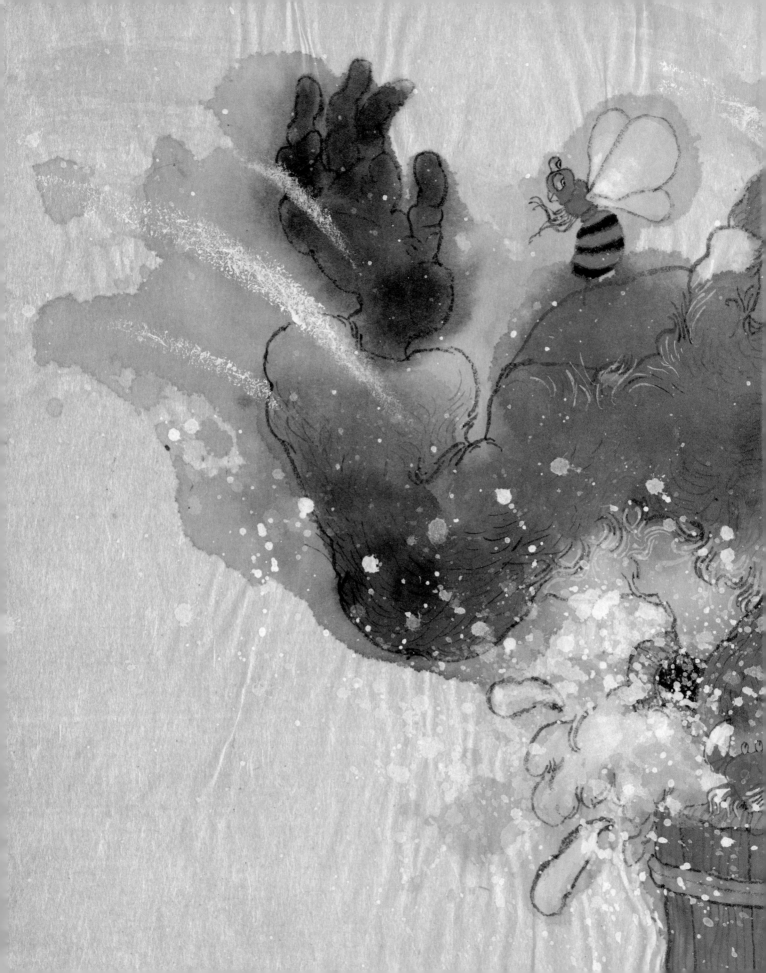

When he leaned over the water tub, the wasp took aim and stung him on his backside. At the same time, all the baby crabs gave a shout and grabbed Mr. Monkey, pinching him with their powerful little claws. "Ouch, ouch! Owww!" cried the monkey, who hurt everywhere.

As he ran out of the house, trying to escape, the monkey stepped on slippery Mr. Cowpat.

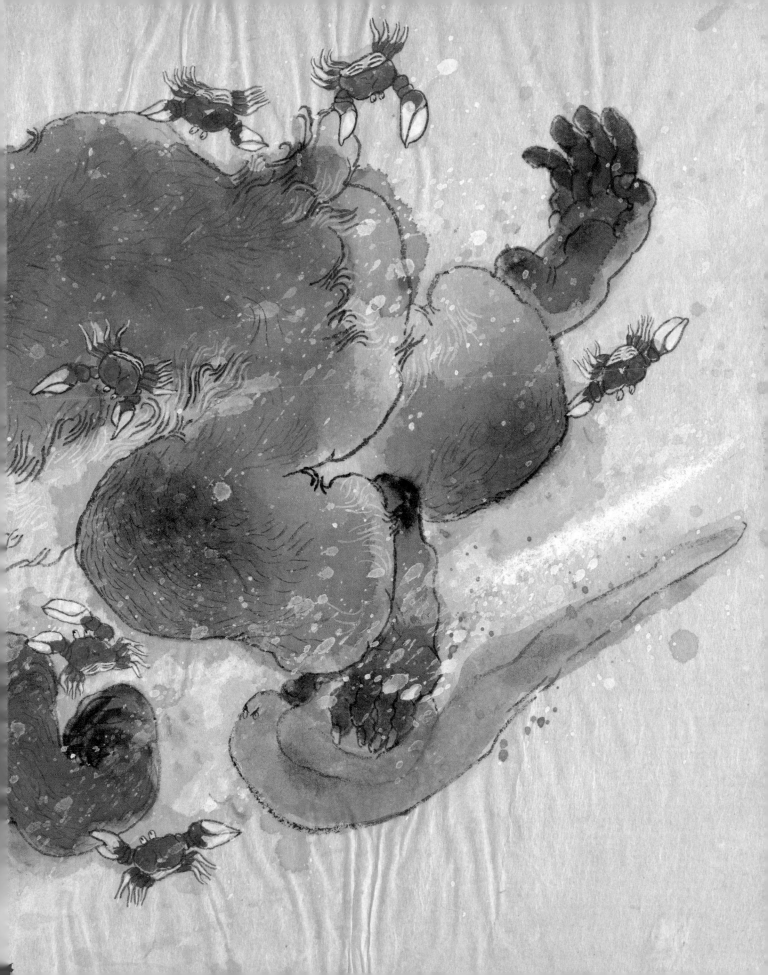

Mr. Monkey slid and fell. At that moment, Mr. Mortar jumped from the rafters. He landed with a thud on the monkey, crushing him with one blow.

"Thank you, thank you, Mr. Chestnut, Mr. Wasp, Mr. Cowpat, and Mr. Mortar!" cried the baby crabs. "Mr. Monkey has been justly punished for his evil acts against our mother!"

AFTERWORD
by Professor Keigo Seki

This is one of the most traditional fairy tales, one all Japanese children come to know. Monkeys and crabs were familiar sights for children living in the Japanese countryside long ago.

The crab's song to the persimmon seed reflects an ancient agricultural rite practiced until quite recently to ensure good crops. At the new year, the farmer would address his persimmon trees, chanting, "Will you or will you not bear fruit? If not, I will cut you down." The farmer then makes a ceremonial slash on the tree trunk while children chant, "I will bear fruit, I will bear fruit!"

There are many variations on the theme of this story; it has been found world-wide in different forms. It bears some resemblance to Grimm's "Bremen Town Musicians," wherein various animals attack evil humans. It is also similar to a South Seas folk tale involving a monkey and a crab who plant bananas. The monkey's banana plant dies due to salty soil on the beach but the crab's banana, planted inland, flourishes. When the monkey eats all of the crab's bananas, the crab fashions a spear at the base of the banana plant that kills the monkey when he descends. Our monkey and crab tale would appear to be a combination of these two story lines.